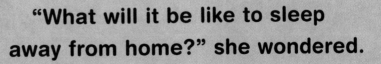

"What will it be like to sleep
away from home?" she wondered.

Magenta packed everything she needed and hurried to Blue's house. Halfway there, she stopped. "Uh-oh!" she cried. "I forgot something!"

"I'm so happy you're here!" Blue exclaimed. "Let's put on a puppet play! Could we use your blanket for the curtain?"

"Um . . . okay," Magenta said slowly.

Blue showed Magenta all of her puppets.
"Do you have a princess puppet?" asked Magenta.
"I always play the princess."

"No," said Blue, "but you could be the unicorn, and I'll be the bunny."

"I know," Magenta laughed, "let's call our play *The Bunny and the Unicorn Have a Sleepover!*"

Magenta and Blue put on a play for Mr. Salt, Mrs. Pepper, Cinnamon, and Paprika.

When it was almost over, Magenta said, "Then the unicorn fell fast asleep under the moon and stars."

"Time for dinner!" said Mr. Salt.
Magenta followed Blue into the kitchen.
"What's for dinner?" asked Blue.

Blue quickly added, "The bunny fell asleep, too, and she dreamed of all the special things she and the unicorn could do in the morning. The End."

The audience clapped and shouted, "*Magnifique!*"

Then Magenta watched the stars twinkle in the sky until she fell fast asleep.

"Good night, Magenta,"
murmured Blue sleepily.
"Good night, Blue,"
Magenta whispered.

"Oh, thank you, Blue," said Magenta. "The stars here look just like they do at home."

Blue and Magenta crawled under the covers.

"I look at the stars and make lots of wishes,"
Magenta said.

"We can do that here, too," said Blue. She opened
the window shade so that they could see the stars in
the night sky.

Magenta covered her
bed with her pink blanket.
"Blue, what if I still can't fall asleep?" she asked.
"Well, what do you do at home to help you go to
sleep?" asked Blue.

"Oh, thank you!" squealed Magenta, hugging her blanket. "Now I can go to sleep."

"Good night," said Mrs. Pepper, turning off the light.

"Good night," Blue and Magenta said softly.

Soon Blue and Magenta were giggling so hard that they didn't hear Mrs. Pepper come into the room.

"Here it is! Good as new!" cried Mrs. Pepper, handing Magenta's clean blanket to her.

"Blue," Magenta said quietly, "I don't think I can go to sleep without my blanket."

"I know how you feel," said Blue. "I don't like to sleep without Polka Dots. Let's tell funny stories until your blanket is ready."

After Magenta brushed her teeth, she sat down on the bed. It didn't feel quite like her bed at home. "I wonder if having a sleepover at Blue's house was such a good idea," she thought.

When they were finished, Magenta asked, "Do you think Mrs. Pepper will have my blanket clean before we go to bed?" "I'm sure she will," said Blue.

Blue brushed her teeth, and then she and Magenta read a story.

"Blue," said Magenta, "at home I read a story first, then I brush my teeth."

Blue thought for a minute. "I know," she said, "why don't I brush my teeth *before* we read the book, and you can brush your teeth *after* we read the book?"

"Great idea!" said Magenta.

After dinner, Blue and Magenta got into their pajamas.
"Is it time for your bedtime story?" asked Tickety.
"Almost," said Blue. "Let's brush our teeth and then
read a book."

"Don't worry!" said Mrs. Pepper. "I'll wash your blanket right away!"

"I hope I get my blanket back soon," Magenta said softly.

"I'm sure it will be clean by the time we go to bed," Blue reassured her friend.

"Would you like some grape juice?" asked Mr. Salt.

"Oh, yes!" said Magenta. "I love grape juice." But as she reached for a glass, she accidentally knocked it over! "Oh, no!" she cried as grape juice spilled all over her pink blanket.

Slowly, Magenta took a small taste of the pizza.
It was chewy and salty and . . . "Delicious!" she cried.
She ate a big piece.

"I usually have plain pizza," Magenta told Blue quietly.
"Oh, I love pepperoni. Give it a try!" Blue encouraged.

"Pepperoni pizza," said Mrs. Pepper.

Magenta didn't know what to do. She wasn't sure if she would like pepperoni pizza.